SUPERDOG

By the same author

SUPERDOG THE HERO
SUPERDOG IN TROUBLE

SUPERDOG

David Henry Wilson

Illustrated by Linda Birch

KNIGHT BOOKS
Hodder and Stoughton

Text copyright © 1984,
David Henry Wilson
Illustrations copyright ©
1984, Hodder and Stoughton
Limited

First published in Great Britain
in 1984 by Hodder and
Stoughton Limited
Knight Books edition 1992

British Library C.I.P.

Wilson, David Henry
  Superdog (Brock red).
  I. Title
823'.914[J]   PZ7

  ISBN 0 340 58008 9

Printed and bound in Great Britain
for Hodder and Stoughton
Children's Books, a division of
Hodder and Stoughton Ltd., Mill
Road, Dunton Green, Sevenoaks,
Kent TN13 2YA (Editorial Office:
47 Bedford Square, London WC1B
3DP) by Clays Ltd., St. Ives plc.

Contents

I
About Me

Hello. I'm Superdog. Well, actually I'm just Dog, but nobody would ever take any notice of a dog called Dog, so I decided to call myself Superdog, and now look – they're writing books about me! I've even got my portrait on the front cover. What a face, what a body! Look at those intelligent eyes, that rose of a nose, that licky pink tongue, those white bone-crunching teeth. Have you ever seen a finer head? It's a superhead, that head. And look at that muscular, hairy body, oozing power from shoulders to tail. There's no doubt about it, I'm the greatest thing to hit the dog world since man invented biscuits.

Now you'd better meet my family. This is Mr Brown. He's a nice man, but as you can see from the worried look on his face, he has a lot of problems. One of his problems is that he can never make up his mind. He'll say things like: 'I'm going to build Superdog a kennel tomorrow.' Then five minutes later he says: 'Maybe I'll do it on Sunday instead.' And later: 'Maybe I won't bother to build one – I'll buy one instead.' And later: 'Perhaps a basket would do.' He just goes on like that, and tomorrow and Sunday both come and go, and I don't get a kennel or a basket. I take Mr Brown for a walk every day so that he can get away from his problems for a while.

Another of Mr Brown's problems is Mrs Brown. She's nice too, but she always makes up her mind very quickly and never changes it. She'll say to Mr Brown: 'Would you put up that shelf today, please?' and Mr Brown will spend all day trying to make her change, but she won't. That doesn't bother me, of course – in fact, I have a good laugh. What does bother me is when she decides: 'It's time that dog had a bath!' It makes no difference to her whether I'm right in the

middle of a bone or a dream or a sniff –
there and then I'm nabbed, grabbed, rub-
bed and scrubbed. Whoever invented soap
and water should have been drowned in the
stuff – preferably before he invented it,
though I suppose that wouldn't have been
possible.

Now I have two special friends: Tony
and Tina. They don't have any problems,

as you can see from their happy faces. They don't have to make up their minds about anything, or avoid doing things someone else has made up their mind about. They can play all day and sleep all night. I think if I could come back to the world in another form, I'd choose to be a child: no worries, always looked after, fed and clothed and warmed and loved from morning till night. It's a funny thing, though – Mrs Brown always says *she'd* come back to the world as a dog. Mr Brown says he leads a dog's life anyway.

There's a lot more things that I ought to tell you about, like our house, our neighbours, our street, my enemy the black and white tom-cat next door, and the beautiful brown-eyed honey of a lady dog that lives four doors away. But I think you'd probably prefer to hear about some of my adventures. Because Superdogs lead very exciting lives, as I'm sure you'll agree when you read on.

2
The Key

Tony and Tina were in bed, and Mrs Brown had gone to a meeting, so I'd been left all alone to look after Mr Brown. We'd been watching television for a while when Mr Brown said: 'Perhaps we'll go for a walk soon.'

I got up and wagged my tail, because that's what dogs are supposed to do when someone says 'walk'. (I think there must have been a slightly deaf dog in the old days who thought 'walk' *was* 'wag', and we've all made the same mistake ever since.)

'On the other hand,' said Mr Brown, 'it's raining, so perhaps we won't.'

I sat down again.

'It's a rotten programme, though,' said Mr Brown, 'and there's a good western later, which I don't want to miss.'

I stood up again.

'Fetch me my shoes, good boy!' said Mr Brown, so I bounded off to the hall to fetch the shoes, which I then carried back into the living-room. And that, I might tell you, was a real act of heroism. Mr Brown has very smelly feet. The only thing that's as smelly as Mr Brown's feet is Mr Brown's shoes, and carrying a smell like that under your own nose requires a lot of courage.

'Good boy,' said Mr Brown again, and gave me a pat. 'We'll just go out for five minutes, eh? Or maybe ten.'

So out we went, and while I sniffed the trees and lamp-posts for signs of Honey, Mr Brown pretended to be very busy twirling my lead, whistling, and shouting 'Here boy!' Honey didn't seem to have been out that evening, but I left her a little reminder of myself on the lamp-post outside her front gate. This was when we were on our way back – Mr Brown having decided that maybe a walk hadn't been such a good idea after all, as it was now raining heavily. And this is the point at which the real adventure begins.

Mr Brown followed me through our front gate (I usually have to show him the way), and we both stood at the front door while he searched for his key. Now Mr Brown searching for a key is like a bulldog searching for good looks, or a Pekinese searching for muscles: the longer they search, the less they find.

'Ugh,' said Mr Brown, 'forgot my key!'

I pretended to be surprised, and gave him a sympathetic wuff.

'Must be here somewhere,' he said, and went through his pockets for the third time, but of course the key didn't must-be-there at all. The key was as much inside the house as we were outside the house, and if we were to join the key in the warm and the dry, it was not going to be through the front door.

I went round to the back door and pushed against it, but it was locked as well.

'I wonder if the back door's locked as well,' said Mr Brown, following me round a minute or two later.

While he tested the back door, which I had already tested, I walked on a bit further to look for open windows. And sure enough, the little window of the downstairs lavatory was open.

'Back door's locked as well,' I heard Mr Brown say.

'Wuff wuff!' I said, to draw his attention to the open window.

'Looks like we're stuck here till Mummy gets home,' said Mr Brown. 'Get ourselves nice and soaked.'

'Wuff wuff wuff!' I said.

'And I shall miss the western as well,' said Mr Brown.

As my wuff-wuffing wasn't working very well, I started woof-woofing, because that usually makes people pay attention, but the only result was Mr Brown calling out: 'No use woof-woofing, old boy. We're stuck and that's all there is to it.'

The thought occurred to me that I might perhaps use my mighty supermuscles to dig a tunnel under the house and up through the floorboards, but any fool could see that it would be much simpler to climb through the lavatory window. Any fool, that is, except Mr Brown. All he would have to do was lift me up.

I bounded across to him, and pulled him by the trouser-leg.

'Hello, Woofer, old boy,' he said. (Everyone calls me Woofer – it's just another name for Superdog.)

I pulled his trouser-leg again.

'Getting hungry, are you?' he said.

Trying to talk to Mr Brown is like trying to make sticks into bones – there's no hope of success. I went to the lavatory window again, and began my famous woof-howl, which not even he could possibly ignore.

'Will you keep that wretched dog quiet!' came a voice from next door's front bed- room window. That's the tom-cat house, and you can tell what nasty, ill-mannered people they are from the sort of words they use. 'Wretched dog' – me, perfection on four feet.

'Sorry, Mr Thomas!' called Mr Brown. 'I've left my key inside!'

'Well next time leave your dog there as well!' said Mr Thomas, and slammed his window shut.

Fortunately, Mr Thomas's rude remarks about my good self had brought Mr Brown right round to where I was standing, below the lavatory window.

'Shush now, Woofer,' he said.

With those lightning fast reflexes for which I am famous, I rushed towards the wall and pretended to climb up it.

'Yes, I'd like to get inside as well,' said Mr Brown.

There are times when even a superdog feels like giving up. But at last Mr Brown looked up and spotted the open window.

'I say,' he said, 'the lavatory window's open.'

I stood on my hind legs, with my front paws against the wall, and looked from Mr Brown to the window and back, whining encouragingly.

'Won't help us, I'm afraid,' said Mr Brown. 'That window's too small for me to get through.'

I whined again.

'Unless . . .' said Mr Brown. 'Unless . . .'

Another loud whine from me – come on, come on, Mr Brown!

'I wonder if you could get the key,' said Mr Brown.

He looked at me, eyes shining with intelligence.

'If I lift you up through the window,' he said, 'do you think you could get the key?'

He made a few turning movements, and said 'Key' several times, as if repeating words would somehow make them easier to understand. I wagged my tail and panted loudly.

'Right, Woofer,' he said, 'key, eh? Get the key. Key, boy, key.'

Then he lifted me up, and I scrambled through the little window. To be more precise, I half scrambled through the little window. My head, shoulders and front paws were in, and the rest of me was out. Mr Brown gave me a helpful shove from behind, which got me three-quarters in, and I could certainly have wriggled the rest of myself through if Mr Brown hadn't decided to give me another helpful shove. I suppose he could only think as far as getting me through the window, and it didn't occur to him that getting through was one thing

3
The Rescue

Courage has always been one of my greatest qualities. A Superdog is never afraid of anything, and whether it's Mr Brown's smelly shoes, or a breakneck climb through the lavatory window, you'll find no hint of fear from me. It's surprising really that I haven't got a whole row of medals pinned to my chest – though perhaps it's just as well, since medal-pinning can be a painful business.

One of my most heroic acts was the rescue which took place during a family outing. It was on a sunny summer's day, and Mrs Brown had made up her mind and Mr Brown's mind that we should all go out for a picnic. We had driven into the country, and parked the car in a field, near a stream. Mr and Mrs Brown laid out the

picnic things, while Tina played with her doll and Tony chased butterflies. I pretended to chase butterflies as well, but I made sure I didn't catch any because I don't trust insects. I chased a grasshopper once, and he jumped straight in my eye, and once when I was very young I thought I'd caught a bee, but in fact the bee had caught me. I was limping for a week after that little game. Superbrave I may be, but I'm also superintelligent, and that means I don't take chances. So if any butterflies are reading this, they can rest assured that they're perfectly safe as far as I'm concerned.

It was after the picnic (juicy chunks of liver in jelly) that I performed my great act

of bravery. We all went for a walk along the bank of the stream. Mr and Mrs Brown led the way, hand in hand and laughing. Then came Tina, still fussing over her doll, which had blue eyes and said Mama. Tony kept stopping to throw stones into the water, and I dashed between all four members of the family, wuff-wuffing to let them know I was still there. None of them took any notice of me, which I found a little hurtful, but then human beings are like that, I'm afraid. One moment they make you think you're the only thing in the world that matters, and the next you might just as well not exist. I wuff-wuffed all the same, because at least the noise reassured *me* that I was still there.

We reached a wooden bridge, and Mr and Mrs Brown stood on it, looking down into the water. Tina and I joined them, while Tony remained on the bank throwing stones. I poked my head over the side of the bridge and looked down. The water was flowing quite fast, and I poked my head back in again, because watching the water made me feel giddy. I don't like heights, and to tell the truth, I don't much like water either. You'll remember the nasty feeling I had had when falling into the lavatory (twice), and baths have the same effect on me.

'Lovely, isn't it?' said Mrs Brown.

'Beautiful,' said Mr Brown.

I looked up at them and shook my head. Human beings have strange ideas about beauty. To look at their faces, you'd have thought they were gazing at a stream of dog biscuits instead of that giddy-making, shiver-shuddering water.

Tina perched her doll up on the side of the bridge.

'Mama!' said the doll.

'Look at Dolly,' said Tina. 'She's sitting on the bridge just like . . . Whoops!'

Dolly had been sitting on the bridge, but Dolly wasn't sitting on the bridge any more. Dolly had dived head first into the water, and we all dashed to the other side of the bridge to see her floating gently away downstream.

'There's your dolly!' shouted Tony, as Dolly floated past him. He threw a stone. 'Missed!'

'You mustn't throw stones at her!' shouted Tina. 'Daddy, Dolly's drowning! She's going to be drowned!'

And thereupon Tina set up a wailing noise that made even my famous woof-howl seem like a whisper in a graveyard.

'Do something, Philip!' said Mrs Brown.

'Right,' said Mr Brown. 'What do you suggest?'

'Wail, wail!' went Tina. 'My Dolly's drow-ow-owning!'

I knew immediately what had to be done.

Someone had to run and catch up with Dolly, dive into the water, and rescue her. If I hadn't disliked water so much, I'd have done it myself, but in the circumstances it seemed to me that Mr Brown should do it.

'Wuff wuff,' I said.

'Ah, Woofer,' said Mr Brown. 'Go on, boy, go fetch Dolly.'

'Not me, you fool!' I wanted to say, but he had already set off in pursuit of the doll, and so I raced after him, and was soon running ahead of him because amongst my other qualities I am a superrunner.

I had soon left Mr Brown far behind, and before long I had even caught up with the doll, which had got hooked on some stones in the middle of the stream. I stood on the bank and barked, while Mr Brown came puffing along in the distance.

From where I was standing, the water looked distinctly wet. Not a pleasant prospect. On the other hand, by the time Mr Brown arrived, and by the time he'd made up his mind what to do, the chances were that Dolly would be off the stones and floating even further downstream. I noticed that there were several rocks sticking out of the water, and with a few lightning-fast calculations, I decided that I could probably step to the doll and back without getting my feet wet.

Very carefully, I set out across my stepping-stone bridge. Actually, it was quite good fun, so long as I didn't look down.

'Well done, boy!' called Mr Brown from the bank.

At least it's nice to be appreciated.

I reached Dolly and picked her up by her dress.

'Mama!' said Dolly, showing how little she knew about life.

'Good boy,' shouted Mr Brown. 'Bring her back! Bring Dolly!'

I would have liked to woof at him that I hadn't come all this way to leave Dolly behind, but with that presence of mind which distinguishes the super from the ordinary, I realised that if I opened my mouth, I *would* leave Dolly behind. And so silently and cautiously I began the dangerous journey back across the rocks. I've seen men and animals making that sort of journey on television, and I wondered if there were any cameras on me.

'Come on, Woofer!'

That was Tina's voice from the bank. They must all be there now, I thought, the whole family watching brave Superdog save Dolly's life. I looked up just to make sure they were all there. And that was my mistake. I had looked up in mid-step, and the foot that had been poised to land on solid rock landed instead on empty air. Down I fell with a splurging splash straight into the icy water.

Fortunately, the presence of mind which I have just mentioned did not desert me. I immediately closed my eyes and kicked out powerfully with all four superlegs, relying on instinct to take me in the right direction.

I am a great believer in instinct. In my

experience human beings tend to think far too much, because the more they think, the less sure they seem to become. Mr Brown is a case in point: he never takes decisions because he's always too busy thinking about what he would miss if he *did* take a decision. I'm more like Mrs Brown myself – I make up my mind straight away, allowing intuition to guide me, and it rarely lets me down. That was why I was quite content to close my eyes and let instinct direct me through the water. In any case, the shock of being in the stream made it difficult for me to force my eyes open.

'This way, boy! This way!' shouted Mr Brown. 'Where's he going?'

He seemed a very long way off. I carefully opened one eye. He *was* a very long way off. I'd been swimming downstream. Perhaps some dogs would have panicked, but Superdogs are made of tougher stuff. I had seen a rock ahead, and with a swift, decisive decision I allowed myself to be swept on to it. And there I remained. The family came along the bank, and Mr Brown called to me to come across and join them, but nothing could induce me to leave the safety of my rock. He who risks his life once is a hero, but he who risks it twice is a silly fool. And I'm no fool. No amount of 'Good boy, here boy, come on boy' rubbish could get me to budge, and in the end Mr Brown was forced to take off his shoes and socks and come paddling out to fetch me.

He carried me back to the bank, and

what a hero's welcome I then received, as they all crowded round me.

'Well done, Woofer,' they were saying. 'Good boy, clever boy, brave boy. Give it here, then, give it here.'

And for some reason they were trying to make me open my mouth.

'Open, boy, give it here.'

It was only then that I realised I was still carrying Dolly. I suppose the shock of falling into the water had made me clench my teeth, and in the terrifying swim that had followed, I simply hadn't opened my jaws again. Of course it was just the instinctive courage of the Superdog. I released Dolly, and allowed Mrs Brown to rub me dry with a towel. Tina wanted to kiss me, and I must confess I did enjoy being made a fuss of. I didn't even have to say 'Wuff wuff' any more, because the whole family knew I was there – even Dolly, though she would keep calling me Mama. I don't think I'd do it again, mind you. But it's the sort of adventure one is always glad to look back on.

4
The Burglar

One of my earliest adventures took place shortly after I'd first come to live with the Browns. I was just a puppy then, but was already filled with that superstrength, supercourage and superintelligence that still amazes me when I think about it. Where does it all come from? How can one dog have so much?

I don't remember very much about the home I had before I came to the Browns, but I do remember very clearly the speech my mother made before I left her.

'Woofer,' she told me, 'human beings are very strange animals. If you do what they want you to do, they'll think you're very clever. If you do what *you* want to do, they'll say you're stupid and stubborn. If you go and get a stick or a stone or a ball, they'll say you're a good boy, but if you go and get a bone or a biscuit or a piece of meat, they'll shout at you and smack you. Always pretend to be stupid, and you can't go wrong.'

My mother was very wise in the ways of the human world. Many is the time that I have begged, panted, tail-wagged, and gazed adoringly into Mrs Brown's eyes in order to obtain those little extras that brighten up a dull day. One longs to say: 'Give it to me and stop messing about,' but mother certainly knew best.

The adventure that I'm going to tell you about arose directly from another piece of advice my mother gave me.

'Human beings,' she said, 'always feel safer when there's a dog in the house. They live in continual fear of something called "burglars". Burglars are other human beings who come into the house and knock people on the head and take their things away. If you ever catch a burglar in your house, your family will worship you for the rest of your life. They'll give you medals, take pictures of you, and show you off to all their friends. Catching a burglar is the most wonderful thing a dog can ever do.'

When she spoke those words, there was nothing more I wanted in life than to catch a burglar. I seem to have changed a little since then. I definitely have no desire to catch a burglar now, and if one did come into the house, I think I would probably pretend I wasn't there. Supercourage is best saved for situations where there isn't too much danger. But in those days I was young and anxious to get on in the world, so I said goodbye to my mother, and went off to the Browns' house, where I waited impatiently for my first burglar.

As it happened, I didn't have to wait long. It was one afternoon when Mr Brown was at work, and the rest of us were in the garden. Mrs Brown was digging in her funny human way, throwing the earth in front of her, and Tony and Tina were playing Mummies and Daddies: Tina was telling Tony to do things, and Tony was not doing them. I was attacking a stick and pretending it was a burglar. Suddenly I heard the side gate of our house open and close. Nobody else heard it, but dogs can generally hear much better than human beings, and superdogs hear things that even dogs can't hear. There were footsteps which were definitely not Mr Brown's. I waited for the man to appear, but the footsteps stopped. He was not coming into the garden. I stood there, ears pricked, head raised, body tense. Mrs Brown had noticed nothing and merely went on digging, and Tina was just smacking Tony on the bottom for saying a rude word. If the burglar was to be tackled, I would have to tackle him myself.

'Catching a burglar is the most wonderful thing a dog can ever do. . . .' It was my big chance. I bounded over the lawn and round the side of the house. And there he was. A small man, with a cap pulled down over his glasses, and the obvious expression of a

man who would knock anyone on the head and take their things away. At the very moment when I saw him, he was in the act of opening a door in our wall, and when he saw me, his eyes filled with a mixture of fear and guilt.

'H . . . hello, boy,' he said.

I let out my lowest, deepest, grumpiest grrrrrrrowl. It's a sound which is so frightening that it even frightens me. The burglar was clearly terrified.

'Now then, boy,' he said. 'Easy, easy.'

The paler, twitchier and tremblier he got, the more confident I became. It was going to be a lot easier to earn the family's worship than I'd expected. All I had to do was make sure this nervous little burglar didn't escape, and I would have medals, fame and love for life.

'Grrrrrrrrrr!' I said again – mainly because I couldn't think of anything else to do.

'Now you just stay there,' he said. 'Sit, boy, sit.'

And he started slowly backing away towards the side gate. I could see at a glance that he was going to turn and run, and that didn't suit me at all. How do you explain to people that you've caught a burglar if the burglar isn't there? I took one of those swift decisions which you have already seen to be typical of me. I charged towards him and bit him in the leg.

'Yaaaaaaaaaaah!' he screamed, and the noise gave me such a shock that I let go and jumped back a dozen paces. Fortunately, I jumped towards the side gate, so that I now stood between the burglar and his escape route. However, he seemed to have forgotten his plan to run away, because he was bending down, holding his leg and moaning.

At that moment Mrs Brown came round the side of the house, followed by Tony and Tina.

'Good heavens, what's the matter?' she said.

'Wuff wuff!' I said, indicating that I'd caught the burglar and was all set to be worshipped.

'He bit me!' said the burglar. 'That x y z dog bit me!' (He didn't actually say x y z but I wouldn't like to tell you what he did say.)

I looked expectantly up at Mrs Brown, waiting for showers of congratulations, medals and biscuits. But all that came down was a hand, and it landed hard and loud on my backside.

'You naughty dog!' she cried. 'Bad dog!

Go to the corner! Go on!'

'Whoo, whoo!' I whined, trying to point out that he was a burglar and I was a hero.

'Bad dog!' she said again, and I slunk away to avoid that hard hand.

'What happened, Mummy?' asked Tina.

'Woofer bit the electricity man,' said Mrs Brown. 'He's a bad dog.'

The burglar had rolled up his trouser leg and now pointed to my tooth marks. 'I might be crippled for life,' he said. 'It could turn poisonous. They might have to cut my leg off.'

'Come inside,' said Mrs Brown, 'and I'll

put some plaster on it. And we'll have a nice cup of tea.'

'I'd better finish reading your meter first,' said the burglar. 'While you're out here to keep him off.'

I stayed in my corner near the fence, and watched him write something in a little book, then go inside with Mrs Brown.

'Poor old Woofer!' said Tina, giving my head a little rub.

'Never mind, Woofer!' said Tony, patting my side.

'I expect he thought the electricity man was a burglar,' said Tina.

I nodded vigorously, and learnt a lesson then which I've never forgotten: human children understand us animals a lot better than human grown-ups.

'Come and play with us, Woofer!' said Tina, and we all went back into the garden.

While we were playing, I heard the side gate click open and shut again, and I heard Mrs Brown saying goodbye to the burglar. Then she came round the house and called to me. I wasn't very keen on obeying her, but I remembered what my mother had said about doing what humans want you to do, so I put on a stupid face and ran across to her.

'Very naughty!' said Mrs Brown, wagging her finger at me. 'You mustn't bite people, Woofer. No biting, eh?'

I would have liked to tell her that if I hadn't bitten the burglar, he would certainly have knocked her on the head and taken her things away, but that wasn't what she wanted me to say. Instead I said, 'Wuff wuff!' nodded, panted, and wagged my tail.

'That's right, Woofer,' she said. 'Good boy. Clever dog.'

The praise wasn't quite what I would call worship, and it wasn't nearly as nice as medals, pictures and piles of dog biscuits would have been. But it was a lot better than a smack on the backside.

5
Honey

Honey is the beautiful brown-eyed lady dog who lives four doors away. It gives me a thrill just to see her shimmying along the street, but unfortunately the people she lives with don't seem to like me very much. Whenever they see me, they pull Honey away, and even if they stop to chat with Mr Brown, they try to get between me and Honey so that we can't have *our* little chat. I can't think why. I've never done them any harm.

Of course it might have something to do with the time when we did have a chat, during our very first meeting. It was a couple of years ago, and I was playing in the garden when I discovered a hole in the fence. With a superwriggle and a super-squeeze I was through the hole and off into

44

the big wide world to seek my fame and fortune. And I got as far as four doors away, where I was stopped in my tracks by this vision of heavenly beauty. She was soft and brown and as tingle-making as a tin of liver and onions. I fell in love with her on the spot.

'Who are you?' she said.

I could hardly believe it – she was actually speaking to me! I looked behind me, just to make sure those gravy-brown, biscuit-round eyes were really directed at me, and then I opened my mouth to reply. At

first I could only let out a gasp and a grunt, because I was so excited.

'What?' she said. 'Speak up!'

'Woof . . . Woof . . . Woofer,' I said.

'Woofwoofwoofer,' she said. 'What a ridiculous name!'

'No, no,' I said, 'just Woofer. Um . . . actually, my friends call me Superdog.'

'Superdog!' she cried. 'You? Superdog? What's super about you?'

At that moment I felt anything but super. I hadn't had much experience of lady dogs, and I'd only mentioned my superness in the hope that she'd be impressed and perhaps ask me to protect her or bury a bone for her or kill a spider or something like that. If I'd known she was going to look down her nose at me, I'd never have mentioned that I was super.

'Well?' she asked. 'How are you super?'

'I'm very tough,' I said, 'and . . . and I'm a fast runner, and . . . and . . . I can do anything. Do you want me to bury a bone for you, or fight a spider . . . ?'

'No, thanks,' she said. 'You don't have to be a superdog to bury bones and fight spiders. Any fool of a dog can do that.'

'Well, I'll race you to the end of the garden,' I said.

'What for?' she asked.

What for? She did ask the most difficult questions.

'Um . . . just to show you how fast I am,' I said.

'Who cares?' she said.

I cared, but if she didn't, then there wouldn't be much point in racing.

'You don't look like a superdog to me,' she said. 'In fact you look like a very ordinary dog. Worse than ordinary. You look common. And stupid.'

'Me, stupid?' I cried. 'Me?'

And I stood there in front of her, with my mouth wide open in the hope that some clever words would find their way into my brain and out through my jaws. But they just wouldn't come.

'Me, stupid?' I managed to repeat.

'Yes,' she said. 'Ordinary, common, and stupid.'

At last I found a good reply.

'Well, I'm not!' I said.

Perhaps it wasn't all that good a reply, but in the circumstances it was the best I could do. She didn't seem impressed, though, and I wished with all my might that I could have the chance to prove to her how tough and brave and strong and clever I was.

No sooner had I made my wish than an amazing thing happened. Honey's eyes suddenly widened from biscuits to saucers, she leapt to her feet, and growled at me as if I'd just stolen her best bone.

'Pardon?' I said, but she growled again, and I could see that those beautiful eyes were round with some sort of fear. Now although I'd wanted to impress her, I certainly hadn't wanted to frighten her, and in any case I couldn't really understand why she should be afraid just because I'd said I wasn't ordinary, common or stupid. I was beginning to think that maybe lady dogs were as unreasonable as human beings, but I thought that at least I should try to smooth things out.

'Sorry,' I said, 'I . . . um . . . didn't mean to frighten you.'

'It's not you, you stupid mongrel,' she said. 'Look behind you.'

I did, and almost jumped out of my own skin. Standing beside the fence, glaring at us with eyes as green as traffic lights, was the black and white tom-cat from next door.

'Well,' growled Honey, 'chase him off. *If* you're such a superdog.'

'Um . . . off?' I said.

'Chase him out of my garden,' said Honey.

This certainly seemed like the chance I'd been waiting for, though I'd been thinking more in terms of spiders, wasps and flies than an animal as big as that tom-cat. Fortunately, there was still some distance between us.

'Um . . . look,' I said to Honey, 'why

don't you go into the house, and leave me to deal with him?'

I would have felt a lot freer if Honey had gone into the house, but she stayed put.

'Chase him off,' she said. '*If* you're so super.'

It was a time for supercourage and super-strength, qualities I have in abundance. I took a careful step in the direction of the tom-cat. The tom-cat arched his back, and I took two rapid steps in the opposite direction.

'Coward!' said Honey.

I am not a coward, of course. How can a superdog be a coward? On the other hand, I am not a fool, and only a fool would start chasing a cat without knowing just how tough and strong that cat is.

Since I had to do something, I began to walk very slowly round the lawn, keeping the same distance between the tom-cat and myself. This was clever thinking, because it would look as if I was taking action, but at the same time I would still be in a good

position to run away if anything went
wrong.

'Coward!' said Honey again. Obviously
lady dogs have no appreciation of clever
tactics.

As I walked, I kept my eye on the tom-
cat, and the tom-cat kept his eye on me. He
hadn't moved at all since I'd started my
walk, and this encouraged me a little. I was
now well away from Honey, and I cautiously eased myself to within whispering
distance of the tom.

'Excuse me,' I mumbled, hoping Honey
couldn't hear, 'but would you mind going

somewhere else? I'd be ever so grateful and . . .'

What happened next was quite extraordinary. Before my very eyes the tom-cat seemed to swell and swell till he was twice the size he'd been before. His fur stood up like bristles on a brush, his eyes blazed like green suns, and he opened his mouth and let out a terrifying hissing, spitting noise which sent shivers through my ears, down my back, and right to the tip of my tail. Well, I just ran. I didn't even know where I was running to, but the next thing I saw was that I was in the street and racing past our very own front gate.

'Hello, Woofer, old chap,' said Mr Brown over the hedge. 'How did you get out there?'

He wouldn't have understood even if I'd told him, but in any case I was much more eager to get inside than I was to explain how I'd got outside. When Mr Brown opened the gate for me, I almost knocked him off his feet, and it was only when I'd actually entered the warm, friendly, tomless place I call home that I stopped running and stopped trembling.

I should think Honey must have been very impressed with the speed of my reactions and of my running, but unfortunately she's never had the chance to tell me so. I sometimes wonder if perhaps the people she lives with are a bit jealous of me, because although Honey is extremely beautiful, her beauty is probably the only superquality she's got. There's no way that she could, for instance, have run away from that cat faster than I did. And I've noticed that human beings like to think that *their* house, children, car, garden etc. are better than everyone else's, so perhaps Honey's people don't like to think their dog is in any way inferior to the Browns' dog.

All the same, I'm still hoping to have another chat with Honey. I expect she'd like another chat with me, too. Perhaps next time, when the humans stop for their little talk, I'll think of something to say.

6

The Christmas Present

Human beings are very strange creatures, and one of the strangest pieces of human behaviour is called Christmas. It's a single day and it comes once a year, and no matter what sort of day it is, everybody is supposed to be happy. The wind might be howling like a pack of hounds, the deep snow might freeze you where you least want to be frozen, and you might be dying of biscuit-lessness or bonelessness, but if it's Christmas Day, you will be happy, and that is that.

I remember my first Christmas with the Browns. I was just a pup, and still innocent enough to believe that things were as they seemed. The family had been talking about it for weeks, and Tony and Tina were especially excited. They kept discussing what presents they were going to get, and Mr Brown was quite excited too, because once he asked me what he should buy for Mrs Brown. I told him to get her a tin of liver and onions, but of course he didn't understand and went and got her a silk scarf instead. I remember that distinctly, because a few days later, when he was at work, she told me what an awful colour it was and the two of us went to the shop to get it changed. Mr Brown never noticed the difference.

A few days before the actual Christmas Day, Mr and Mrs Brown carried a spiky green tree into the living-room. At first I thought this must have been for my benefit, because it had become very cold outside. However, when I went up to the tree and gratefully raised my hind leg, they very quickly made it clear that the tree was not, so to speak, for my convenience, and I was rushed out at great speed.

The next event was the decoration of the tree and of the living-room. The children

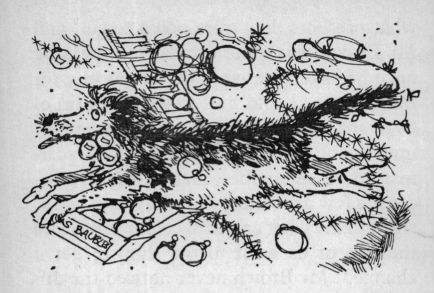

helped their parents to stick silver balls and coloured paper and flowers and berries all over the place, and I helped them by carrying things round the room. Well, at least I meant to help them. Only I couldn't help wondering what sort of flavour those silver balls might have, and when I tasted one it accidentally got stuck in my throat and I had to be carried out again so that I could cough it up. Nowadays, being a little older and wiser, I keep out of the way when there's any decorating going on. It's not just the silver balls that are worth avoiding, it's also the hammers that fall on your head, the feet that trip over your body, and – as happened on one occasion – the ladder that suddenly gets in your way, with Mr Brown on top of it.

It was during the decorating, when I had returned from my battle with the silver ball, that Tina asked a very important question:

'What,' she asked, 'are we going to give Woofer for Christmas?'

Until that moment, Christmas had appeared to be none of my business, but now I became very interested indeed.

'Ah,' said Mr Brown, 'we hadn't thought of Woofer, had we?'

Perhaps *he* hadn't thought of Woofer. Personally, I think of Woofer all the time.

'Well,' said Mr Brown, 'maybe I'll build him that kennel I've been meaning to build. Though that might be a lot of work. No, maybe I won't. I don't know. What do you think, darling?'

'I hadn't thought of Woofer either,' said Mrs Brown. 'But I expect I'll have had an idea or two before Christmas.'

'There you are, Woofer!' said Tina, giving me a hug, 'you'll be having a Christmas present, too!'

And with all the enthusiasm of youth, I went racing round the living-room with loud wuffs of excitement, until I accidentally knocked against a coffee-table which was underneath a vase of flowers which was full of water which splashed all over me and the carpet as the vase came crashing down. Mrs Brown wasn't very pleased, and I left the room for the third time.

All through the days that followed, I kept wondering what my present was going to be. I listened in to every conversation, and I watched everything that came out of Mrs Brown's shopping bag, and I sniffed at every parcel that found its way under the Christmas tree . . . but nothing sounded, looked or smelt like a present for Woofer. I even began to think they might have forgotten me after all, but the day before the great day I heard Tony ask Mrs Brown if she'd bought something for me. My ears almost leapt off the top of my head.

'Yes,' said Mrs Brown.

'What is it?' asked Tony.

I went hot and cold all over.

'You'll see,' said Mrs Brown.

And that was *all* she said. The excitement was really unbearable. Even an ordinary dog would have found the suspense too much, and as a young, superintelligent, supersensitive, extraordinary dog, I simply couldn't contain myself. So I did a diddle on the hall carpet.

After that I went into the kitchen and pretended not to know anything about anything, but somehow Mrs Brown guessed that it was *my* diddle, and I had the usual thump on the bottom and a long, finger-wagging lecture. How did she *know* it was my diddle? It always seemed unfair to me that I was automatically the one accused. I mean, it could have been the children, couldn't it? Or Mr Brown.

Anyway, I must get to the real point of

my story, which is the events that took place that night and the following morning. As you can imagine, it was quite impossible for me to sleep, and I simply lay in my basket trying to guess what my present might be. Clearly it would not be something I had normally, which ruled out bones, tins of meat, dog biscuits, and – I hoped – baths and tellings-off. On the other hand, there was very little that I really wanted apart from nice things to eat. So it gradually became more and more certain in my mind that my Christmas present would be food of some sort. The next question was where Mrs Brown would hide it. Well, for a brilliant brain like mine, that presented no difficulty at all. Where do you normally hide food? Obviously, in the kitchen.

I crept into the kitchen. By the light of the moon I opened the pantry door and had a good old nose around, but there was nothing special in there. I opened the various kitchen cupboards, and I even managed to pull open the drawers in the cupboards, but there was nothing except pots and pans and papers and packets and brooms and brushes and cans and cutlery and . . . stupid, boring things that couldn't possibly be a present for a Superdog or any other dog.

I'd almost given up when I came to the oven. Something about the oven made me stop, sniff, lift my nose in the air and sniff again. There was a smell in there that was definitely quite different from all the other smells in the kitchen – sweeter, juicier, meatier. . . . That was the sort of smell a Superdog might expect from his Christmas present – the sort of smell that made a Superdog want, more than anything else, to get the oven door open. And as luck would have it, I knew that the catch had broken a couple of weeks ago, because Mrs Brown kept on asking Mr Brown to mend it, and Mr Brown kept on saying he would, but didn't. He had simply tied it together with some string, and with my supersharp teeth I had no trouble at all in biting through that. Click! The oven door swung open almost at my touch. And oh, the smell that came out! How can I describe it to you? It was the sort of smell that went in through your nose, made its way straight down into your mouth, and wandered around there tickling all your teeth and your tongue and your jaws until they simply oozed with hunger. I had never been so hungry in all my life.

And the cause of the smell? Roast turkey. I couldn't believe it. A whole roast turkey, big and brown and yum-suck-crunchy as yum-suck-crunchy can be. What a present! Oh, I could there and then have bounded up the stairs, rushed into the front bedroom, and kissed Mrs Brown a thousand times – only I didn't, because there was something else that I wanted to do even more. No dog, no living creature could have resisted that smell. I got my head inside the oven, buried my teeth in a turkey leg, and pulled the whole yummy bird out and down on to the kitchen floor. The metal tray it was on let out a loud clatter, and for a moment I froze in case the noise might wake somebody up. But the house remained still, except for the smell waves reaching out, and my taste waves meeting them halfway.

You may say that I should have waited until the next day to enjoy my present, but you must remember that I was very young, and young dogs are never as patient as old dogs. Besides, I only intended to take a few mouthfuls, and it *was* my own present, and it surely wouldn't make any difference to the Browns though it would certainly make a difference to me. I tucked into my turkey,

and believe me, nothing had ever tasted better. Christmas, I decided, was one of the best ideas human beings had ever had.

I suppose I had munched and scrunched my way through about half my present before I began to feel rather full and just a little sick. The only thing to do was to lie down and have a good sleep, and I remember the last blissful thoughts that I had before I dozed off. I was the luckiest dog in the whole world, and roast turkey was the best present any dog had ever had, and although the Browns might be a little disappointed that I'd discovered my present before Christmas Day, there was no point in trying to put it back in the oven, and in any case they'd probably laugh and say what a clever dog I was to have found it . . .

Only they didn't think I was clever, and they didn't laugh, and I was not the luckiest dog in the world at all. On the contrary. When Mrs Brown came into the kitchen the next morning, her cry of rage and horror not only woke me but it practically turned me into a lump of marrowbone jelly. I've never been so terrified in my life. Her cries brought Mr Brown, Tony and Tina racing downstairs, and it was clear from all their faces and all their reactions that the fuss was not caused by disappointment at my finding my present too soon. The turkey wasn't my present. The turkey was their Christmas dinner.

Well, how was I to know? I tried to explain to them what had happened, but I knew they'd never understand. Perhaps Tony and Tina did, because they both said it wasn't my fault, and later in the day Mrs Brown did say it was partly Mr Brown's fault for not mending the oven door, but that thought certainly didn't occur to her when she woke me up with her angry, horrified voice. And it didn't occur to her right through the morning either – a period which I spent in the garden shed, recovering from a nasty bout of shock and acute indigestion.

However, by the afternoon they had

decided to forgive me, and Tina was allowed to carry me back into the house. That was when the last twist of the story took place. You see, Mrs Brown *had* brought me a Christmas present. It was a rubber bone. Now I ask you, a rubber bone! Can you think of anything more disgusting than a rubber bone? And imagine chewing a rubber bone after you've just chewed half a roast turkey! The very smell of it made me feel sick. But, as I've said so often before, human beings are quite impossible to understand, and if they were angry at me for enjoying the best Christmas present in the world, I knew – even at that tender age – that they would love me for pretending to enjoy what was definitely the worst. So I chewed the rubber bone, wagged my tail, panted, and rolled my eyes.

'There you are,' said Mrs Brown. 'He likes it.'

Well, if you have to be happy on Christmas Day, then you have to be happy.

7
The Supermarket

Shopping is not my idea of a treat. Going along a busy street with Mrs Brown is like trying to run through a forest of moving trees. I'd have no trouble on my own, but being tied to a lead I'm a ready-made victim for stabbing high heels, bruising toecaps and scrunching boots. And even when we get to the shops, either I'm not allowed in, or I'm kept on such a tight lead that I feel like Mrs Brown's third shoe.

Mrs Brown often goes to something called a supermarket. You'd have thought a supermarket would be the ideal shop for a superdog, but even there I get tied to a post and left to watch life go by. I used to try howling, growling, straining, jumping, but in the end I found that the best way to get noticed was to sit perfectly still with my tongue hanging out, looking as helpless and pathetic as possible. Then one or two people would come along (usually children), pat me on the head, and tell me what a nice doggy I was.

But I haven't been to the supermarket for a few weeks now. I suspect it's because of what happened on my last trip there. As usual, I was sitting nice-doggily beside my post, looking hopefully up and down the pavement. After several patless minutes, I noticed two boys coming towards me – they were quite a lot older than Tony and Tina, and the moment I saw them I knew they were baddies. I can always tell at a glance which humans are dogly and which are undogly, and I only needed half a glance to see that these boys were very undogly indeed.

As they drew near, I removed my expression of aren't-I-sweet and replaced it with watch-out-I'm-dangerous. They stopped a couple of paces away, gazing straight at me, so I let them have my menacing growl, which I found pretty terrifying even if they didn't.

'Don't look too 'appy, does 'e?' said one.

'No,' said the other.

'Don't like bein' tied up, that's 'is trouble,' said the first.

'Yeah,' said the second.

''E don't wanner sit there all day, does 'e?' said the first.

'No,' said the second.

'So we oughter untie him an' let 'im run off,' said the first.

'Yeah,' said the second.

Now this didn't seem a bad idea, though I couldn't quite work out how two bad boys could come up with an idea that wasn't bad. So as the first boy leaned down and untied my leash, I gave him a sort of grateful menacing grunt and put on a nice-dog, nasty-dog expression. You can't be too careful with humans.

'C'mon,' said the first boy, 'let's gerrout of 'ere.'

'Yeah,' said the second boy, and the two

of them walked quickly away as if they'd just done something wrong.

Freedom! It was a great feeling. There was no limit to the things I could do. If I wanted to, I could now walk up the street, or down the street, or across the street, along the pavement, or in the road, into the shops, round the shops, out of the shops, past the shops . . . the choice was endless. So what did I choose in the end? Naturally, I chose to go into the supermarket and give Mrs Brown a nice surprise.

I walked up to the supermarket door, which actually opened itself to let me in, and there I stood for the first time in paradise. Oh, those nose-tickling smells –

fruity, meaty, fishy, sweety, milky, cheesy (or was it feety?) – and those eye-filling sights: boxes and bottles, cans and cartons – shelf upon shelf upon shelf of sheer delight. I wandered down one of the lanes, totally lost in the wonderment of it all. How could Mrs Brown have left me outside when heaven was here within?

'What's that flaming dog doing in here?'

The voice came like a clap of thunder out of a clear blue sky. It was a rough, rude voice, instantly recognisable as the voice of an undogly baddie. And when I looked round, there he was, huge and red-faced (*he* was flaming even if I wasn't), bearing down on me with the look of a man about to murder a dog. What could such a creature be doing in paradise?

'Come here, you little brute!' he cried.

With those lightning reflexes that have so often saved my adventures from unhappy endings, I raced away from his clutching hands.

'Grab him, Sandra!' he shouted.

Sandra must have been the young lady ahead, with narrow eyes and wide arms. By now I was barking at the top of my voice, in the hope that Mrs Brown might hear me and come to my rescue.

'Come on, boy,' said Sandra, but any friend of the flaming man's was no friend of mine. A quick feint to the left and a shimmy to the right and I was past her and sprinting down another lane. Things were looking desperate. It was a typical human trick – show a dog a bone, and then kick him when he's looking at it. (Not that the Browns would ever do such a thing, but I've seen it happen. And not just to dogs. You ask the wasp in the jar, the mouse in the trap, or the fish on the line. Not that they deserve any better, but you can see what I mean, can't you?) Well, they weren't going to catch *me*.

Where *was* Mrs Brown? Or where was the door?

'Grab that confounded dog!' yelled the voice. 'Martin! Sandra! Catch him!'

Of course he didn't quite know what he

was up against. But then, on the other hand, nor did I. And I didn't want to find out. Superspeed and superdodge were the qualities I needed at that moment, and fortunately I have plenty of both. I didn't quite succeed in dodging an old lady's shopping basket, but although all the contents went flying, I didn't even stumble. On I went with a woof and a whoosh. It takes more than a shopping basket to stop me when I'm panicking.

It was the same with the pile of tins which I sent rolling in all directions – I scarcely even felt the bump, though the people running after me did, because I heard one of them fall over and shout something rude.

In one of the lanes I ran down, I suddenly spotted my dinner. Or rather, row upon row of my dinners. And row upon row of other dogs' dinners, as I could see from the different pictures on the tins. (None, I'm pleased to say, as good-looking as me.) I stopped for a moment, to look at all that liver and mince and chicken and beef . . .

'Grab him!' they yelled.

You see, they'll fill their shop with your dinner, and then murder you for standing in front of it.

I shot round the nearest corner, and was just about to race down the next lane when a different voice rang out. It was a voice that I knew very well:

'Woofer!' it said. 'Come here at once!'

It was a voice I would never dream of

disobeying. It was the voice that called me for breakfast, dinner and supper every day of my life. No voice had ever sounded sweeter to my ears than that voice at that moment. And no dog ever obeyed more promptly than Woofer at that moment.

'Sit!' said Mrs Brown. I sat.

The flaming man arrived.

'Is this *your* dog, madam?' he asked, between puffs and blows.

'Yes,' said Mrs Brown, 'he is.'

'Dogs are not allowed in the shop, madam!' flamed the puffer and blower.

'I know,' said Mrs Brown. 'I left him outside, but he must have got loose.'

'We have big notices on all the doors!' blew the flaming puffer.

'Unfortunately my dog can't read,' said Mrs Brown.

'Under no circumstances are dogs allowed in here!' puffed the flaming blower.

'I'll write it down for him so he re-members,' said Mrs Brown. 'Come along, Woofer, let's get you outside.'

The flaming man walked with us all the way to the door, constantly mumbling about notices, damage, licences and control, and trying his hardest to step on me as we walked. In fact, when we finally reached the door and he stopped to see us out, his legs were only inches away from my jaws.

'I'm really very sorry,' Mrs Brown was saying, 'but it was an accident . . .'

And just then my jaws somehow seemed to have a mind of their own, because they opened, fixed themselves on to one of the flaming man's legs, and then closed again. It tasted a bit like cheese.

'Aaaaaargh!' cried the flaming man.

'Come along, Woofer!' cried Mrs Brown.

I never knew Mrs Brown could walk so fast. For a moment I thought she must be a superhuman, but I don't suppose there's any such thing.

Since then I've never been back to that supermarket. I've got a funny feeling Mrs Brown hasn't either.

8
Holiday

I'm going to tell you about the worst experience I ever had. Even now I go hot and cold just thinking about it, and I hope I shan't suffer too much in retelling the story.

It began with a short discussion. Mrs Brown said: 'Where shall we go for our holidays this year?' Mr Brown said: 'I don't know.' And Mrs Brown said: 'France.'

That was the end of the discussion. It didn't mean anything to me until a few weeks later, when the news came out that I would not be allowed to go to France. Tony and Tina were very upset at this news, and so was I. Why couldn't I go? they asked, and Mr Brown came out with some long words which I couldn't understand. I still don't know why they couldn't take me. Perhaps this France was some kind of supermarket, full of flaming men who didn't like dogs. But then how could anybody even think of going there for a holiday?

What was to become of me, then? Who was going to take me for walks, brush my coat, open doors when I wanted to diddle? AND WHO WAS GOING TO FEED ME? I could already see myself lying stretched out on the floor in an empty house, thin, dirty, and slowly starving to death. The vision made me feel quite ill. Tina must have seen how miserable I was, because she put her arms round me.

'Who's going to look after poor Woofer?' she asked.

'Aunt Meg,' said Mrs Brown.

'Aunt Meg!' cried Tony. 'Oh no, poor old Woofer!'

'He'll just die!' wailed Tina, which didn't exactly cheer me up, I can tell you. I had no idea who this Aunt Meg was, but if Tony and Tina didn't like her, then I wouldn't either, and I certainly didn't fancy dying at her place any more than I fancied dying at mine. I let out a heart-breaking whine.

'Can't we go somewhere else for our holiday?' begged Tina. (I often marvel at how well she reads my mind.) But no, it had all been arranged, and in any case when Mrs Brown's mind is made up, she never un-makes it. It was to be France for them and Aunt Meg for me, and no amount of Tony/ Tina pleading or Woofer whining could change the terrible plan.

When the dreaded day came, I lay in my basket feeling half dead, and pretending to be completely dead.

'Come on, Woofer old chap,' said Mr Brown.

I let out the sort of moan I imagined a dead dog would let out. Mr Brown didn't seem to notice how dead I was – he simply carried me to the car, and off we went, with Tony and Tina taking it in turns to give me cuddles and sympathy.

Aunt Meg looked like a giant two-legged Pekinese. She had a fat squashed-up face with a lot of grey straggly hair that flopped down on either side of it. I hated her straight away, and I could tell from the tight way she held my lead that she hated me. As the family drove away, I tried to run after them, and nearly strangled myself.

'No, you don't,' said Aunt Meg. 'You're staying with me.'

'Urk, urk!' I gasped, as she dragged me into the house.

As soon as she banged the front door shut, I did a diddle on her hall carpet. It was the least I could do. She saw what I was up to and slapped my behind, so I bit her in the hand. Thereupon she got down on all fours, pushed her squashy face right up against me, and bit me in the leg. She did! When I think about it, I go weak at the knees. The shock, the pain, the humiliation! I hardly knew where to put myself, I felt so insulted. In any case, she didn't give me a chance to put myself anywhere. Before I could even examine the wound, she'd grabbed my collar and yanked me through the kitchen, out of the back door, across the garden, and ll the way into the garden shed.

'That's where you stay,' she announced, till you've learned how to behave yourself.' The door shut, and away she stomped.

Till *I'd* learned how to behave myself! What about her? Since when have human beings been allowed to bite dogs? I sat there in the gloom of the shed, twisting my head round in all directions to see what damage she'd done to me. I could just make out the teeth marks at the top of my right front leg. I was lucky she hadn't bitten clean through it. Even now I might lose the leg – after all, who could tell what horrible diseases a human being might give a dog?

I sat there in that shed I don't know how long. My companions were a lawnmower, a wheelbarrow, and a whole lot of tools and pots and boxes. At one moment a spider scuttled across the floor almost under my paws, but I was too shaken and miserable even to trip him up. Tina had said I'd die at Aunt Meg's, but even she couldn't have foreseen the awful nature of my death. How

could the Browns have done this to me?
Hadn't I always been the nicest, kindest,
lovingest faithfullest friend to them?
Hadn't I suffered Mr Brown's smelly slip-
pers, Mrs Brown's painful baths, the disgusting taste of rubber balls, the constant
misunderstandings, Mr Brown's failure to
build my kennel, Mrs Brown's failure to
reward me for burglarbiting, and so on and
so on, always with a cheerful wuff and a
fixed look of contentment? What more
could they have asked?

I let out a mournful howl, and I hoped
they would hear it in France. It was a sound

I'd never actually made before, and it certainly had an effective ring to it. I tried it again. A howl like that would travel for miles. Tina would hear it for sure and would shed a few tears for me, and perhaps even Mrs Brown would hear it, realise I was dying, and make up the family's mind that they must return at once.

But the only person who seemed to hear my howl was Aunt Meg. I heard her footsteps a long way off, and by the time she'd opened the door, I'd squeezed myself under the wheelbarrow and was giving a brilliant imitation of a dog who wasn't there. But she saw me. She had evil powers, Aunt Meg.

'Lunchtime, Woofer,' she said.

If Mrs Brown had said those words, I'd have been out of the shed like a stone out of Tony's catapult, but an invitation from Aunt Meg was like an invitation to a murder. Mine. I had no intention of letting her take another bite at me.

'Ah well, please yourself,' she said, and the door closed again.

It was only now that I realised how hungry I was. With all the emotional upset of leaving the Browns, the mental upset of being abandoned to Aunt Meg, and the physical upset of being bitten, my stomach was as hollow as half a tennis ball. I crawled out from under the wheelbarrow, and scratched at the door to see if it would open. It wouldn't. I gave a few of my famous woof-howls to see if I could bring Aunt Meg back. But I couldn't. I was not going to die from a Meg bite after all. I was going to starve to death, and I would never see food, daylight or the Browns again.

You might think that being a superdog I would have forced my way out of that shed, but I couldn't. It was solid wood all over, and specially built to withstand even my superstrength. This would have to be a matter for brains rather than muscles. I tried the mournful howl instead of the woof-howl. No response. I tried some whining and whimpering. Still no response. I tried grunting and growling, snarling and snuffling, woofing and wuffing, but Aunt Meg didn't come. In the end, I simply lay down and went to sleep.

It worked. The next thing I knew was that the door had opened, the sun was shining in, and a beautiful smell was floating up my nostrils.

'Thought you'd died in here,' said Aunt Meg, 'you were so quiet.' (Yes, going to sleep *was* a clever idea.)

In case you've misunderstood me, the beautiful smell was not Aunt Meg. She was worse than Mr Brown's feet. No, the nose-sweetening came from the dish she was carrying – my very own dish. My jaws started to tingle as the smell drew nearer and nearer.

'Liver and onions,' said Aunt Meg, as if I didn't know.

It was the best meal I'd ever had. I enjoyed it so much, Aunt Meg could have bitten me twenty times and I'd never have noticed. In fact I didn't even know she was still there till I scrunched the very last mouthful and happened to look up.

'That wasn't so bad, was it?' she said. Then she picked up the bowl in one hand and my collar in the other, and I meekly accompanied her into the house.

'How about a drink?' she said.

I had my drink.

'And now,' she said, 'we'll go for a little walk. Since you've learned how to behave.'

We went for a walk.

And that was how things were from that day onwards. Whatever she wanted, I did, and whatever I wanted (like diddling on her furniture, biting her hand, or woof-howling in her ear), I didn't do. Instead, I wagged

my tail and put on my nice-doggy face. And so I got my meals and my walks, and remained mercifully unslapped and unbitten. 'Always pretend to be stupid,' my mother had told me, 'and you can't go wrong.' Did any mother ever give better advice?

If the first day with Aunt Meg was the worst of my life, the last day was certainly the best. When the doorbell rang and I heard Tony and Tina's voices, I nearly knocked over even the giant Pekinese as I rushed into the hall.

'Calm down!' she said, but nothing could keep me back from that door, and as soon as she opened it, I was up and licking. What a reunion it was! I was hugged and stroked and patted till my back was quite sore, but even then I didn't want them to stop.

'How have you two been getting on, then?' asked Mrs Brown.

'Splendidly,' said Aunt Meg. 'He played up for an hour or two on the first day, but I soon showed him who was boss and after that he was as good as gold.'

'He certainly looks happy enough,' said Mr Brown.

'That's because *we're* here,' said Tina.

'I think he'd be happy to stay with me for another fortnight,' said Aunt Meg. 'Wouldn't you, Woofer?'

I pretended not to hear.

'Well, we'd better be off,' said Mr Brown. 'See if the house is still standing.'

Then they all said their goodbyes, and Mrs Brown thanked Aunt Meg for looking after me, and Aunt Meg thanked Mrs Brown for the present they'd brought her, and Mr Brown thanked Aunt Meg, and Aunt Meg thanked Mr Brown, and Tony refused to kiss Aunt Meg, and Tina didn't want to kiss her either . . . It was all very jolly.

At last we were away, leaving Aunt Meg standing in the doorway, giving us a cheerful wave. I'd like to have seen her face when she went back into the hall. I'll bet she wasn't so cheerful when she saw what I'd left on her carpet.

Another Knight Book

David Henry Wilson

SUPERDOG THE HERO

The Brown family call him Woofer, but he
sees himself as Superdog. And when it
comes to fighting daffodils, cricket balls and
a runaway cow, he's certainly a superhero.
Honey, the beautiful lady dog, and the
black and white tom cat next door, might
find it hard to believe, but as Woofer
himself says 'That's the great thing about us
superdogs — nobody ever knows what we'll
be up to next. Not even me.'

The second book about the inimitable
Superdog.

Another Knight Book

David Henry Wilson

SUPERDOG IN TROUBLE

Woofer, or Superdog as he is better known,
is a super-clever and very brave dog —
according to him. But his attempts to prove
it always seem to go disastrously wrong:
running away from home, trying to impress
Honey, the beautiful lady dog, or even just
lying by the fire, poor old Woofer can't help
getting into trouble. Only his Superdog
skills can bring him out on top . . .

The third book about the inimitable
Superdog.

Eric Thompson

DOUGAL STRIKES AGAIN

Dougal and his friends must raise two
million pounds to save the garden from a
motorway. There's only one solution —
Dougal must get a job . . .

Six hilarious stories about the much-loved
characters from The Magic Roundabout.

Also available: The Misadventures of Dougal

Another Knight Book

Rev. W Awdry

BELINDA THE BEETLE

Belinda is a little red Volkswagen Beetle and
as soon as Susan and John and their parents
see her in William Whisker's garage, they
know that she's the only car for them. But a
gang of thieves is interested in the little car
too — what can they be after?

An exciting adventure from the author of
the Thomas the Tank Engine books.

Also available: Belinda Beats the Band.

MORE GREAT BOOKS AVAILABLE
FROM KNIGHT